ZION BENTON PUBLIC
LIBRARY DISTRICT
Zion, Illinois 60099

DEMCO

JANNA
AND THE
KINGS

BY PATRICIA SMITH
ILLUSTRATED BY AARON BOYD

LEE & LOW BOOKS INC. · NEW YORK

Lee & Low Books Inc., 95 Madison Avenue, New York, NY 10016
leeandlow.com

Manufactured in China

Book Design by Tania Garcia
Book Production by The Kids at Our House

The text is set in Sabon
The illustrations are rendered in watercolor

10 9 8 7 6 5 4 3 2 1
First Edition

Library of Congress Cataloging-in-Publication Data
Smith, Patricia.
    Janna and the kings / by Patricia Smith ; illustrated by Aaron Boyd.— 1st ed.
        p. cm.
    Summary: Janna loves the Saturday visits that she and her grandfather make to
the local barbershop where she becomes a princess, but after he dies, Janna feels
as though her world has changed.
    ISBN 1-58430-088-4
    1. African Americans—Juvenile fiction. [1. African Americans—Fiction.
2. Grandfathers—Fiction. 3. Death—Fiction.] I. Boyd, Aaron, ill. II. Title.
PZ7.S9418 Jan 2003
[E]—dc21   2002067114

For Mikaila, the perfect granddaughter,
the happy ending to all my stories
—P.S.

For the Old Man and Frieda
—A.B.

J anna heard Saturday before she saw it. Still in bed, she listened to Mama's singing rise over the pop of bacon in the skillet. No bells on clocks went *brrriiing*. There was no warning from Mama to "Girl, stop pokin' so slow or you'll be late for school." There was just the music of a no-school morning and the smell of bacon and eggs tummy-tickling from two rooms away.

Janna yanked open dresser drawers and pulled out jeans, kneesocks, and a strawberry-colored T-shirt. Granddaddy would be knocking on the door any minute, and if she wasn't ready to go, he would settle down in the kitchen with Mama. Then they would start talking about the good old days when Mama jumped double dutch and Granddaddy had all his hair.

"You certainly are jumpy this morning," Mama said when Janna ran into the kitchen. "Going somewhere?"

Mama had a teasing way of saying things she already knew.

Janna's baby brother, Rashid, squeezed a lump of fried egg through his fingers. He goggled his eyes at Janna and screeched, "Hanna!"

"Jan-na," she said slowly, so Rashid's ears could get used to the sound of her name.

Rashid laughed, flashing his two teeth, and pointed at Janna with a slice of bacon. "Hanna!" he cried again.

Janna was so excited, she hardly tasted her breakfast. She didn't even squirm when Mama worked the tangles out of her hair and twisted it into two neat braids. By the time she heard Granddaddy's footsteps on the porch, Janna's head was full of thoughts about how much fun the day was going to be.

"Hey, Princess Sugarlump," Granddaddy said, picking up Janna and whirling her around until the sweet spin made her dizzy.

Granddaddy was Janna's best friend in the world. She loved the way he looked, his arms and legs skinny as pick-up sticks. She loved his voice, which was smooth and growly at the same time. She loved how his hair looked like cotton candy snow. But most of all Janna loved how they spent every single Saturday together.

Walking down Madison Street with Granddaddy was like strolling a kingdom with a king. Granddaddy knew everyone, and his real name, Otis, was everywhere in the air. He and Janna joked with the firefighter. They said hello to Mr. and Mrs. Green, out for their morning walk. Janna saw Kaila, her second best friend after Granddaddy, and Tata Chip, a dog that belonged to everyone and no one, romped in a rain puddle. Janna bent down to scratch his wet belly.

Granddaddy bought a cup of coffee for himself and an apple muffin for Janna, and they sat at a folding table on the sidewalk outside Watson's corner store.

"So, Princess Sugarlump, what should we do today?" Granddaddy always asked the same question.

"I think you need a haircut, Granddaddy," Janna always answered even though he didn't really.

"You know, I believe I do," Granddaddy replied as he always did. Then he finished his coffee, Janna took a last bite of muffin, and they headed for her favorite place in the whole world—Terrell's barbershop.

The morning was warm and the door to the barbershop was open. Janna took a deep sniff of the sugary smells of shampoo and aftershave and that oily spray that made cut hair shine like diamonds.

Then Janna heard the voices coming from inside the barbershop. There was laughing and teasing and bragging. The room was full of kings, just like Granddaddy.

As soon as Janna and Granddaddy walked in, the words "pretty" and "sweetheart" and "there's our baby" washed over Janna and made her feel like a real princess. Amos, who played the organ in church, gave Janna a hug, flashing his bright gold tooth as he smiled. Mister Odell, who worked in the meat market, and Terrell, the barber, who talked all the time and never seemed to take a breath, were there also.

Janna's seat was an old kitchen chair beneath a black-and-white picture of Terrell taken back when the shop was new. The breeze from outside made balls of cut hair dance across the floor, and the three big leather barber chairs looked just like thrones. There was always lots of talking, and no matter what the kings talked about—baseball, the old days, a TV show—they always, *always* asked Janna what she thought.

"Let's see what Princess Sugarlump has to say about that," Mister Odell would declare. Then they would all stop and listen because, as Granddaddy always said, she was a princess and everything a princess had to say was important.

One day, right before Saturday rolled around again, Janna
awoke to the sound of her mother on the telephone. Something
was wrong—her voice was too high and her words came too
fast. They made Janna hug her pillow as tightly as she could.

When Mama came into her room, Janna couldn't look at her.
She just stared at her pillow while Mama hugged her tight and
told her that Granddaddy's heart had gone to sleep.

The king had left his princess without saying good-bye.

Lots of Saturdays passed, but to Janna they didn't feel like Saturday anymore. There were no steps on the porch, no knocks at the door, no sweet and dizzying whirl-arounds.

Rashid played busily with his toys. "Janna!" he called, loud and clear, but Janna didn't hear that he had gotten her name right at last. Even though Granddaddy was gone, time kept moving on.

One Saturday morning Janna began walking down Madison Street the way she had always gone with Granddaddy, just to see if the world missed him as much as she did. She said soft hellos to people she met, and they said soft hellos back. Tata Chip wagged his tail in greeting, but Janna walked by without petting him. She stopped for an apple muffin, but its taste made her lonely.

No one asked Janna what she thought they should do today.

Janna walked past Terrell's barbershop three times. She heard the voices and sniffed the sugary smells, but it didn't feel right to go in without Granddaddy. Too much had changed. She was only a princess when a king held her hand.

Janna was sure that she didn't belong in the barbershop anymore. If she went in, the other kings would ask what she wanted, and she wouldn't be able to tell them she wanted her best friend back. She wanted Saturday to sing its old song.

Janna walked slowly toward the barbershop once more, but this time she stopped in the doorway. She stared at her feet and kicked the welcome mat with her toe.

The voices stopped.

"Well, if it isn't Princess Sugarlump," Amos said in that big booming voice of his. It felt strange to hear just one voice instead of all the voices at once. Janna saw Amos smiling at her, his bright gold tooth winking hello over and over again. She saw the kings and the deep lines in their faces, lines that grew deeper the harder they smiled.

The sun behind Janna seemed to be pushing her into the barbershop. She stepped inside, and it felt like Saturday again. Her chair was still there beneath the old faded picture. Terrell took Janna's hand as he motioned for her to sit.

Then all the kings' voices reached Janna at once—Mister Odell's, Terrell's, Amos's. The words "pretty" and "there's our baby" and "sweetheart" washed over her, just as they used to.

Janna kicked her feet and grinned up at the familiar faces gathered around her. Slowly she began to feel like a princess again. Granddaddy wasn't gone. Janna could feel him here among the other kings, in this place they both loved.